To Mom and Dad

SIMON & SCHUSTER BOOKS FOR YOUNG READERS • An imprint of Simon & Schuster Children's Publishing Division • 1230 Avenue of the Americas, New York, New York 10020 • Copyright © 2016 by Kristyna Litten • Originally published in 2016 in Great Britain by Simon & Schuster UK Ltd. • First US edition 2016 • All rights reserved, including the right of reproduction in whole or in part in any form. • SIMON & SCHUSTER BOOKS FOR YOUNG READERS is a trademark of Simon & Schuster, Inc. • For information about special discounts for bulk purchases, please contact Simon & Schuster Special Sales at 1-866-506-1949 or business @simonandschuster.com. • The Simon & Schuster Speakers Bureau can bring authors to your live event. For more information or to book an event, contact the Simon & Schuster Speakers Bureau at 1-866-248-3049 or visit our website at www.simonspeakers.com. • Book design by Tom Daly • The text for this book is set in Matchwood WF Std. • Manufactured in China • 0815 SUK • 10 9 8 7 6 5 4 3 2 1 • CIP data for this book is available from the Library of Congress. • ISBN 978-1-4814-6154-2 • ISBN 978-1-4814-6155-9 (eBook)

BLUE & BERTIE

KRISTYNA LITTEN

A PAULA WISEMAN BOOK

SIMON & SCHUSTER
BOOKS FOR YOUNG READERS

New York   London   Toronto
Sydney   New Delhi

Every day Bertie and the giraffes did the same thing at the same time. *Crunchity-crunch*–they nibbled sweet leaves from the tops of the trees.

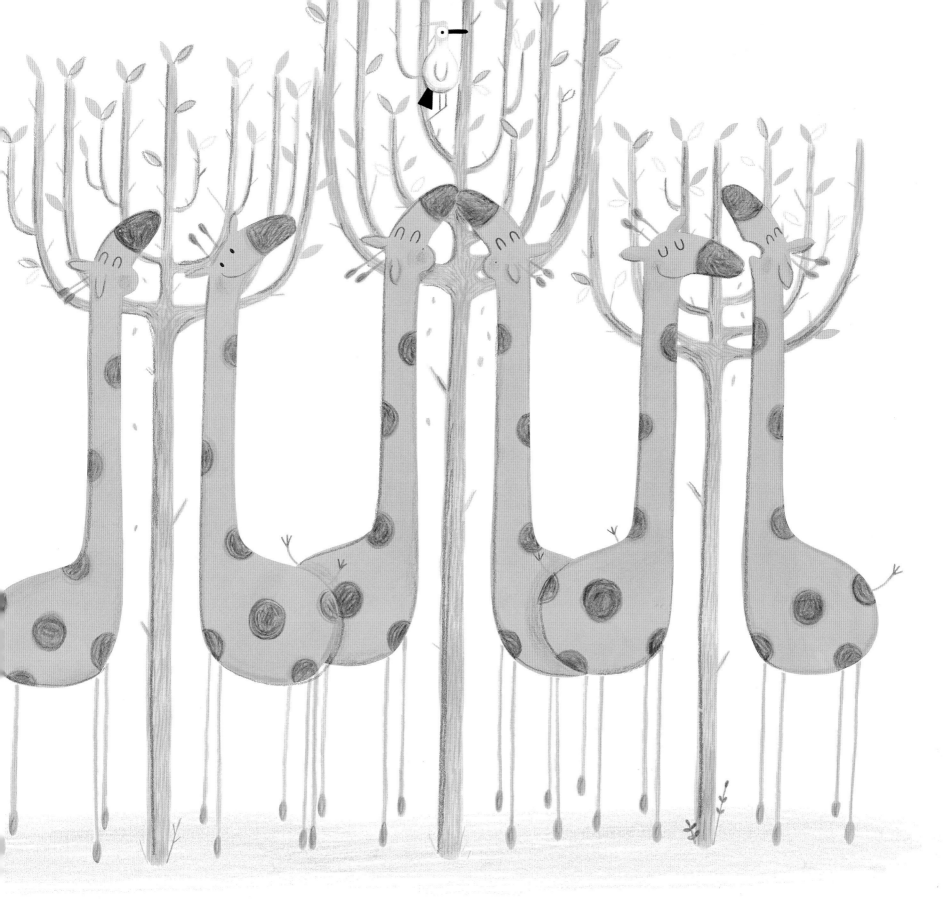

Sip, slurp–they took a cooling drink at the watering hole.

And when they were tired, they
curled their long necks, and —
snore, snore, snore —
they snoozed.

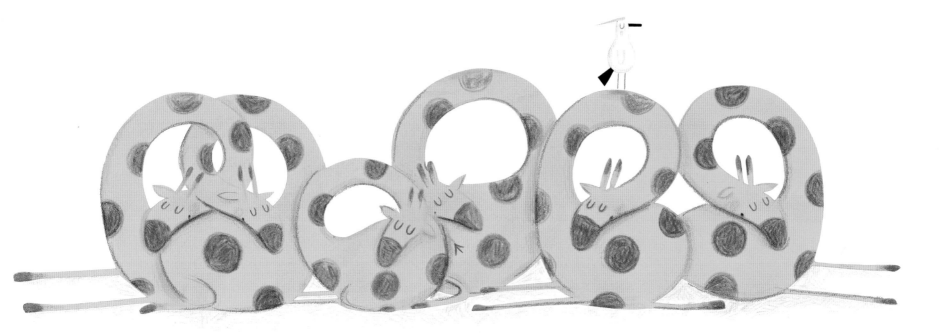

Each day was much like the last,
and that was just how they liked it.

Crunchity-crunch.
Sip, slurp.
Snore, snore, snore.

And then, one day . . .

Bertie overslept!

When he woke up, he realized he was alone.

He'd never been on his own before.

"What should I do?
What should I do?" said Bertie.

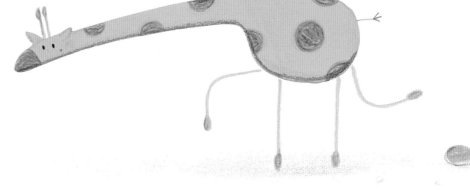

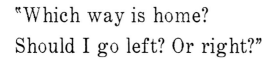
"Which way is home?
Should I go left? Or right?"

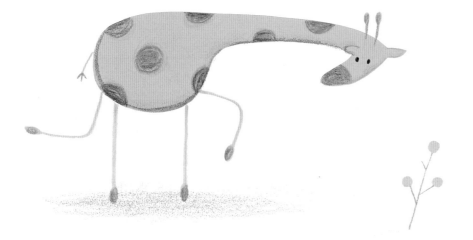

"Where is my herd?
Straight ahead? Or back?"

Bertie was lost.

Soon big, salty tears were rolling down his cheeks.
How was Bertie going to get home?

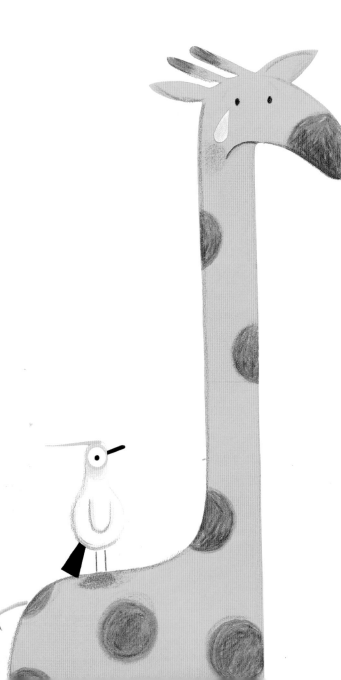

Suddenly, he heard a noise.
"Hello?" he said. "Who's there?"

"I can see you," said Bertie bravely. "And I'm not afraid."

"I am a little bit afraid of you, though," said the creature, stepping forward shyly.

Bertie was amazed.
The creature was just like him, only he was BLUE.

"Don't be silly," said Bertie at last.
"There's nothing to be afraid of.
I'm just a lost giraffe."

"My name is Blue," said the
creature. "I can show you
the way home if you want me to."

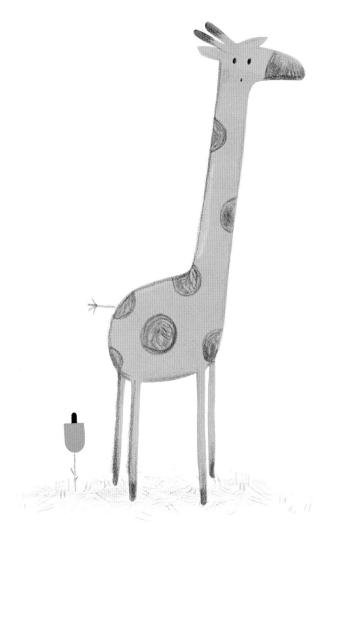

So – *trit trot, trit trot* – off they went together.
"You all right, there, my friend?" asked Blue.
"Very all right," said Bertie. "I never
knew all this was here!"

Trit trot, trit trot—
on they went.

"Look at all this!"
said Bertie.

"These are the rarest
flowers in the world," said
Blue. "Come, there's more
I want to show you!"

Gallopy-gallopy-gallopy – whoosh!
"I feel free!" cried Bertie.
"You are free, my friend," said Blue.

"I never knew there was so much to see,"
said Bertie. "Thank you, Blue."

"Why don't we do it again
tomorrow?" said Blue.
"I can't," said Bertie. "I have to *crunch,*
sip, and *snore* with all the others."

"Oh," said Blue sadly.
"Well, in that case . . .

. . . your herd is just over there."

"Yes, it is!" said Bertie.
"Hello! Hello! It's me.
I'm home, everybody!"

"Bye, Bertie," said Blue, and he turned to leave.

"Blue, wait!" called Bertie. "Aren't you coming?"

Blue hesitated.
"But I don't belong," he said.

"Trust me, my friend, you do,"
said Bertie.

Bertie was right.
The herd loved Blue, just the way he was.

From then on, the herd still *crunched* and *sipped* and *snoozed*. But now they saw things a little bit differently each day.

And that was just how they liked it.

And Blue and Bertie
remained the very best of friends.